This book belongs to:

_____

D1060090

Shabbos is Coming!

We're LOST in the ZOO

By Devorah-Leah
Illustrations by Maya S. Katz

Dedicated to the Friends of Ohr Somayach

Just like people, some of the animals
in this book call the Sabbath
by the name of Shabbat. Some call it Shabbos.
By whatever name you call it,
may you find it just as sweet!

This book is dedicated to
all our boys, with all our love,
M.S.K, D.L.G.

© Copyright 1998 by The Judaica Press, Inc.
All rights reserved. No part of this book may be reproduced
or utilized in any form by any means electronic or mechanical, including
photocopying, recording, or by any information storage
or retrieval system without written permission from the publisher.

10 9 8 7 6 5 4 3

Library of Congress Catalog Card Number: 98-27872

ISBN 1-880582-32-5

Printed in Hong Kong

THE JUDAICA PRESS, Inc.
123 Ditmas Avenue, Brooklyn, NY 11218
718-972-6200   800-972-6201   JudaicaPr@aol.com
http://www.judaicapress.com

**Moshe and Sarah
once went to the Zoo
to see all the creatures
who came two by two**

to the Ark Noah built
that had sailed on through
that terrible flood
'til the skies turned blue.

Moshe and Sarah
got lost in the Zoo.
Now it's almost Shabbat.
Oh, what shall they do?

They can't find the path
and it's making them dizzy.
They pass every cage
and each creature is busy,

because Shabbos is coming,
and there's so much to do.
Only once in a week
Shabbos comes to the Zoo.

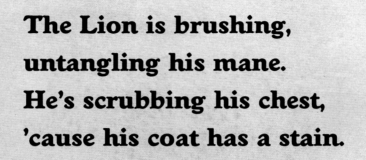

The Lion is brushing,
untangling his mane.
He's scrubbing his chest,
'cause his coat has a stain.

"Can you show us the path?"
says Moshe, "We're rushing."
The Lion can't hear him.
He's too busy brushing.

The Leopard's arranging
and washing her spots.
She's combing her tail
and checking for knots.

"Oh Leopard, excuse us,
but what's the way home?"
The Leopard just whistles
and washes her comb.

The Camel is warming
the food on his hump.
Instead of a table,
he sets a tree stump.

"Can you show
us the path?
We're so tired
of looking!"
The Camel
says, "Humph!"
and goes on
with his
cooking.

The Owl is sharpening
and shining his beak,
mumbling, "Whoooo said what
in the Torah this week?"

"Oh Owl, we're late!
We don't know what to do!"
The Owl just winks
and answers, "Whooo...whoooo."

The Tigers are clipping
and cleaning their nails.
The Donkeys are sweeping
the floor with their tails.

The Parrot can't answer
the children. Instead he
says, "Shabbos is coming!
I have to get ready!"

"Which way?" Moshe calls
to the birds in their bath.
"Tweet! Ask the Giraffe!
She can show you the path!"

But who ever heard
of a talking Giraffe?
From high overhead
came the sound of a laugh

"Each creature is given
one mouth, but two ears.
A person should speak
half as much as he hears."

"Now, my job every Friday
is watching the sun.
So I tell the whole Zoo
when Shabbat has begun."

"Can you show us the path?"
Sarah asks with a tear.
"I can see the whole city
from way, way up here!

"I can see the nice spice cake
your Mama just made.
It's a treat for Shabbat!
You'll be late, I'm afraid.

"And that wouldn't be right.
No, that just wouldn't do!
The path begins here!
Now get going, you two!"

Moshe tossed a banana
to a chattering monk.
He bit it in half
and then threw back a chunk

saying, "Thanks for the snack,
but I've no time to eat!
I must shampoo my belly
and polish my feet.

"I'm only a monkey,
but, in my own way,
I like to make Shabbos
my loveliest day!

"So thanks for the snack,
but it's already late!
You'd better get going.
Now head for the gate!"

But which way?
The Elephant pointed his trunk.
"If we didn't keep Shabbos
the Ark might have sunk!

"I've been hosing my cage down
the whole afternoon.
Now it's past four o'clock
and Shabbos comes soon.

"You've been playing with us
since a quarter to two.
Don't you think you've had
enough time in the Zoo?"

Goodbye to the Elephant,
Monkey, Giraffe...
The children got home
just in time for their bath.

"Children!" their mother said,
"Where have you been?
It's only an hour
'til Shabbos comes in!"

"A tall friend, a fat one
a small one who chatters,
reminded us we have
more interesting matters

"than playing with friends,
when the sun's nearly setting!
We're sorry we're late
and we won't be forgetting

"the lessons we learned
when we went to the Zoo.
We're glad we have Shabbos.